MOUNTAIN MAN CANDY

FRANKIE LOVE

For Hazel,
This one's for you, love!
xo,
frankie

Clive is the local man candy in his mountain town. But after tragedy struck years ago, he's closed himself off to the idea of love.

It's gonna take someone extra sweet to break his hard-candy shell.

When candy-maker, Hazel, moves into town, he finds what he's been waiting for.

But falling in love means more than just satisfying a craving and he has to weigh the filthy-sweet rewards to decide if he's ready.

Dear Reader,
Mountain Man Candy is more than a short and sexy sugar-rush.
It's a romantic AF, sprinkles on top, dipped-in-chocolate-cherry
that's about to be popped, bite-sized piece of perfection.
It's a mouthful--and you deserve the extra calories. Promise!
xo, frankie

COCKING A BROW AT THIS BROAD, I decide to give it to her straight.

"Look, I don't do solo trips," I tell her. "I suggest you book a private rafting trip with Charlie if that's what you're looking for." I lean over the counter and hand her my buddy's card. "Call him—or better yet, FaceTime him. I can guarantee he'll answer that call."

"But you are the one I want… the one every woman wants. At least that's what everyone was saying at the bar last night."

I scowl, hating her reference to me being the local *man candy*. A nickname I can't seem to shake. Before I'm forced to say anything more, Charlie walks into the office.

"What's going on in here?" Charlie asks, his eyes darting between Tanya and me. I step away from the counter, raising my hands. Not wanting anyone to think I am even slightly interested in this woman who is coming on way too strong.

I refrain from saying she wants a booty-call, even though that is exactly what she wants. "Tanya here is looking to book a private rafting trip. Thought you might be able to take her."

Charlie's eye rake over Tanya and her too-tight shorts and barely-there top. I know Charlie likes what he sees. And the truth is, he'd never turn down a few days in the woods with a willing woman.

Linesworth is a vacation destination—a small Bavarian village in the valley of the Washington State Forest. And our company, Forest Expeditions, is busy most of the year with tourists. At least, I call them tourists; Charlie calls them hook-ups. Mostly though, we take out families or older couples on trips. I know he'll see a woman like Tanya as a treat.

I push away from the counter as Charlie takes over booking his fling. Sitting at my desk, I pull up a web browser and go to the real-estate listings I'm constantly scouring. This town is getting crowded, and I want to buy more property on the outskirts before some developer swoops in and buys up everything that's good about these mountains.

As I run my hand over my beard, I see more of the same. A few places to lease locally, a few ridiculous McMansions, but nothing like I want. A big piece of land where I can build a home. A property large enough for a garage that could hold all my outdoor gear. I was about to buy something a few years ago, but then my brother-in-law, Luke, had his accident and well, things changed. Being close to town for my sister became more important than my dreams of getting away from the crowds. Moving into her guest house was the right thing to do. God knows, Luke would've done the same for me.

Not that I have a family. Not that I ever will. Hell, no. I saw firsthand what his death did to my sister and her kids, No way in hell would I risk doing that to a woman. My job is dangerous and I don't want to live any other way, but no woman deserves to get the call that a trek went wrong and now she's a widow.

So I keep my head down. And no matter how many women ask for my number, I refuse to give it to them. It's not because I'm an asshole—it's because I never want to put myself in a position where I might break someone's heart by dying way too soon. Hell, I'm no virgin, but it's been a long-ass time.

But now I'm itching to carve out a space of my own. Maybe not move there full-time, but at least put down a foundation for a house.

My phone buzzes. It's a text from my sister Greta.

Can you watch the kids for a few hours? Maggie can't help and I've got to finish an order.

I look up, seeing Charlie with his arms wrapped around Tanya. He'd better not charge her for their weekend together. I text Greta back right away, knowing if our sister Maggie can't help, I need to step in. And hell, I want to—those kids mean the world to me.

I text back. *Of course, drop them off at the office.*

Ten minutes later, my apron-clad, covered-in-flour sister is waving goodbye and jumping back into her Subaru.

Charlie pulls away from Tanya when he notices my niece and nephew are about ten feet away.

"Lucy! Milo! What are you doing here?" he asks, a big smile on his face. He may be a manwhore, but he loved Luke like a brother too. Hell, the three of us started this business together.

"Mama has to work." Lucy crosses her arms. "So Uncle Clive is watching us. Although I think I'm big enough to watch myself."

Giving her a serious look, I bend down to her level. "You may be big enough, but Milo's only four. He needs us. And we need him." These two kids are the only people on this planet that can turn me into a softie and I'm proud of that.

Lucy twists her lips, deciding whose side I'm on. "You're right. This little guy does need us." She ruffles her little brother's hair and he pushes her away.

"Who you calling little?" He furrows his brow, just like his dad did and damn; it kills me sometimes to think that Luke will never see Milo grow up.

Still, his words get us all laughing, even Tanya who has managed to slip her arms back around Charlie's waist.

"On that note, let's get out of here," I tell them. "I've been cooped up all day."

Lucy frowns. "It's only eleven in the morning."

But for me, even one hour in an office is one hour too long.

"I heard there is a new candy cart in town," Tanya tells us. "Just opened today."

I frown. "You from around here?" I was born and

raised in this town. I'd think I'd know if a new business was opening.

Tanya rolls her eyes. "Look, I was just being nice. I saw it when I was getting coffee this morning."

"Aww, be nice to Clive," Charlie says. "He's not used to talking to pretty girls."

Ushering the kids out the front door, I scowl. "I talk to them plenty, I just don't want what they're offering."

With the kids gone, Charlie is more liberal with his obnoxious, I-only-get-away-with-this-because-I've-know-you-forever, jabs. "You never want what anyone is offering."

"What's that mean?" Tanya asks, pulling herself up on the counter like she belongs here. Exactly who the hell is this woman?

"It means Clive hasn't hit anything in years. Hasn't had his whistle—"

I cut him off, narrowing my eyes. "You're messed up, you know that, right?"

He just laughs and I wave him off. We have been friends since we were kids but I don't exactly need him advertising my sexual dry spell to the goddamn world at large.

Outside the shop, I take Milo and Lucy's hands and then head down Main Street.

"What's Charlie talking about in there? What didn't you hit?" Lucy asks, skipping as she walks.

I take a deep breath, ready to walk back in the shop and whack Charlie over the head. "He's talking about the fact I'd never hit anything or anyone."

"Of course, you wouldn't," says Milo. "Cause even

though Mama says you're hard in the head, we know you're as soft as a teddy bear."

They have a point, because the next thing I know, I'm being led toward the new candy cart in the town square, and God knows I don't have a sweet tooth.

Chapter 2

HAZEL

My motto has always been when life gives you lemons add some sugar, some gelatin, and whip up a batch of jelly beans. I mean, the hard, sour bits of life are always gonna be there. Always. But it's all about perspective.

And right now, despite the fact I'm scraping by with exactly two hundred and twelve dollars in my business and checking account combined—I'm still standing here, on my own two feet, on the first day of my new life.

Though, to be perfectly honest, the morning has been a bit slow. Well, more than a bit. I've sold four lollipops, one bag of sour-drops, and have smiled so sweetly, so much that I think my mouth might go into a sugar-coma. Which is saying something for a woman with a sweet tooth.

I readjust my white apron for the hundredth time. The apron I made in my cramped apartment in Seattle before I took a leap of faith and drove East in an attempt to live my dreams. Exactly one week ago.

The apron I hand-embroidered—because one thing a girl learns when growing up with nothing besides her bootstraps—is that if you want something in life, you have to make it happen on your own. So, I stitched the name of my candy business in bright pink letters all by myself: Sweet Dreams.

I don't have a shop of my own, yet. Right now I have a cart I built thanks to a YouTube tutorial and about four hundred trips to the home improvement store.

But one day I will have a shop of my own. I look down Main Street of the town I visited once as a girl and thought was the most magical place in the world. Not that I'd been many places in the world—but in my ten-year-old mind, the mountain-walled hamlet was everything my childhood wasn't. The wooden balconies and two-toned timber frames of the houses made the village cozy and cheerful. A place that made me feel like anything was possible. The sweetest of dreams.

And one day, I'll have a proper shop on Main Street. Complete with a kitchen in the back so I don't have to rent space at the local commercial kitchen. A place where I can have open shelving, holding rows of big glass jars stocked with every brightly colored candy I can concoct. One day.

But before all that pie-in-sky-dreaming becomes reality I need to sell more than twenty dollars' worth of lollipops.

Smile, Hazel, I tell myself. Be as sweet as the candy you're selling.

I reach below my cart and grab a bin of rock candy

on a stick hoping if I fill that canister to the brim it might look more appealing to customers.

"Miss," an older woman asks, waving her wallet around. "Do you take cards?"

I grin and nod, and she begins filling her arms with all sorts of pretty treats. Rainbow fudge and gumdrops and sweet tarts. Bags and bags of each.

When I add up her total I feel my shoulders drop for the first time in forever. This is what hope feels like. If I have five sales like this each day, I'll be able to afford the guest house I'm renting, because while I've paid first and last, I need to make enough sales to afford the months in between. And ten sales like this would mean I could pay for utilities and groceries. And twenty sales? That would mean I could start saving for my shop.

But I need to treat every customer like my best customer, not get lost in my daydreams. We chat for a few minutes as I bag up her treats and swipe her card on the reader attached to my phone. My first debit transaction!

And it seems like customers draw more customers because before I know it a few more tourists find their way to my cart and purchase an item or two.

The sun is shining and it's after eleven a.m. which I realize, is probably when people are more in the mood for sugary sweets. An adorable little girl runs to the cart, her eyes wide with wonder, her blonde curls bouncing as she jumps up and down.

"I want it all," she moans dramatically. "Just look at all these goodies!"

"Slow down, Lucy," a man says coming up behind

her, holding the hand of a younger boy. The boy is pretty adorable, but the man himself… wow!

He makes my cart look pitiful. Truth is, he's the epitome of man candy. We're talking a walking sugar rush. Biceps that make me want to be his Baby Ruth. I may be a twenty-three-year-old confectioner, but under the apron and honeyed smile, I have all sorts of ideas about what I could dip in chocolate.

And yes, I know that's naughty, but one look at him and I know he is what my sweet dreams are made of.

The little boy tugs on his arm and I remember that I am not in a man-candy factory and am, in fact, a respectable businesswoman. "Can I have a jawbreaker?" the little guy asks.

"I don't know what your mom would think of that, Milo."

"Aww, she won't be mad. You can just explain that we were hungry."

The little girl faces the boy, who happens to be her spitting image. And with their light hair and bright blue eyes, they look just like the man with them. I swallow. My personal lollipop preference is their father.

"It'll break your teeth. Get something softer, goose," the little girl says.

I try not to let my misjudgment get in the way of a potential sale and I smile widely, pushing out the idea that I want to lick this mansicle. Well, actually his *pop*sicle. He is a father after all.

I bite my bottom lip. I am so entirely inappropriate.

These children have a mother. And I am not her.

I am not a part of this familial equation.

But oh, my gosh, this girl called her little brother goose. These kids are just too adorable.

Turning my attention from the dad and laying it on with all-natural, organic cane sugar (no HFCS here!), like I initially intended, I point to a more suitable choice for the little man.

"How about the snakes?" I ask, pointing to a jar of six-inch gummy serpents.

Milo's face lights up. "That's perfect. Lucy hates snakes."

I look at their father, and he just shakes his head. Pointing to the jar beside it, he says, "And you're scared of spiders. Suppose Lucy gets those to torment you?"

Milo pushes his lips forward, thinking it through. "True. I promise to not let one bite you, 'kay Luce?"

She smiles at him, then standing on her tiptoes she looks at each jar, debating her choices. "I want the candy necklace."

"All right," their father says. He may be a married man, but my eyes can't help but look at his rear as he reaches for his wallet. Not wanting to be a creeper, I take out cellophane bags and package the candy for the kids. "I'm Clive, by the way. I work down the street at Forest Expeditions."

"I'm Hazel." I bite my bottom lip, immediately imagining myself going on an expedition with him. Getting lost in the woods. Oh, my gosh, get it together! "And I work here, obviously."

He smiles, but it doesn't stretch wide across his face. He may be *unintentionally* sending hot-tamale signals to every woman on this street—and yes, I've been watching. Every lady is checking him out. I can respect him for not engaging in the I-want-to-break-my-jaw-on-you vibes, considering he is married.

And with the next sentence out of his mouth, it's clear his mind is certainly on her.

"Should we get your mom something?" he asks.

Lucy and Milo smile and my heart warms that he thought of getting his wife something. It's no surprise that I'm pretty much in love with the idea of a man who is a sweetheart.

"What is her favorite candy?" I ask him.

He frowns and then shrugs. "I have no idea."

I hold my tongue. How can a husband not know what his wife likes?

"Maybe something sour?" He looks at Lucy.

She shakes her head. "Mama hates sour anything."

"That's not true," Milo argues. "She likes the lemon tarts Auntie Maggie makes."

Lucy crosses her arms. "Not really. She just pretends she does."

Not wanting them upset over nothing, and wanting to help turn them into loyal customers I suggest my grown-up line. "I have these champagne bears and peach Bellini hearts. Maybe your mother would like them?"

Lucy giggles. "Champagne!" She grins. "That's perfect for Mama. She has a shirt that says Rosé All Day."

"Even better, I have Rosé Roses." I pull out the rosette-shaped gummies. "Pink roses are my favorite flower, and these candies are pretty much perfection."

Lucy nods, agreeing. "Now that that's settled. What about something for your dad? We don't want to leave him out."

Immediately Lucy's face crumbles and Milo looks at her with a heavy frown.

I look at the man in front of me not understanding my error.

"We don't have a daddy," she says. "Not anymore."

The man clears his throat. Takes a deep breath. He leans closer to me and quietly says, "Their dad, he uh, died three years ago."

"Oh my gosh, I'm so sorry…"

He cuts me off. "It's okay. You didn't know."

I look down at the kids who are watching our exchange. "Well, um, should we get your, um, your..." I realize I don't know how Clive fits in with the kids. Is he their mom's boyfriend, their nanny, their neighbor?

Lucy helps me out. "We should totally get Uncle Clive something. He doesn't like Rosé though. You like whiskey, right?"

He ruffles her hair as if wondering where she comes up with this information.

"What?" she asks laughing. "He does!"

I exhale, relieved that she helped me out of that one. He is Uncle Clive. Though the kids mentioned an aunt. He could still be married.

"Whiskey? Hmmm... Don't have any of that. The closest I've got to that is root beer."

"I'm good, actually," he says, looking at the ground, the ease of our conversation gone. I feel terrible for bringing up a tough topic with the kids, and him—all of it. "Just ring these three up and we'll be going."

As I turn to ring up the order, a woman my age stops by and asks Clive if he has plans Saturday night.

With a curt nod, he says he's busy. She frowns and then adds, "If you keep saying no to every date you'll be single forever."

She pats his arms and leaves and Lucy looks up at him, giggling. "You should have a girlfriend, Uncle Clive. Don't you ever get lonely?"

I hand Clive back his debit card with a flutter in my belly. So, he is definitely single.

A few moments later they walk away, and I can't resist checking him out. His ass is finer than any I've seen, and his sweet cheeks soften the cold hard fact that he doesn't give me a second look. In all honesty, I don't think he hardly gave me a first glance either.

He may be man candy, but it appears that his jar is on a shelf I won't be able to reach anytime soon.

Chapter 3

CLIVE

The last time I woke up hard and horny was, well damn, I don't know. Charlie was right. It's been a long-ass time since I had a woman in my bed.

After all the shit that went down when we lost Luke, the idea of being close to a woman terrified me. I know all too well what happened to my sister after her husband died and I swore I'd never put a woman through that pain. Sleepless nights, years of work with grief counselor appointments, tears at the most unexpected times.

But damn, I can't sleep worth shit. My mind is filled with images of that sweet-ass candy girl, Hazel. Her body was all curves and her smile lit up that damn candy cart—which is saying something. Everything she sold was bright and colorful.

And it wasn't just the way her jeans hugged her apple-shaped bottom or her big, round breasts that were poorly concealed by her apron. No, it was how damn sweet she was with Lucy and Milo. How she appeared genuinely upset for mistaking me as their father.

She may have been eyeing me like she wanted a piece of my man candy, but she wasn't over-the-top about it, which is refreshing in this town. Most women here don't seem to give a damn that I'm not interested. But Hazel didn't seem interested in anything except making sure she hadn't offended the kids.

I may not have been overly talkative when I stood at her cart, but damn, I most certainly am captivated. But I know that will lead to nothing but trouble. So I push her out of my mind, roll over in my bed, and try to sleep.

It doesn't work. Next thing I know my cock is hard, in my hand, and I am dreaming of Hazel. Of her luscious lips kissing mine, of her soft skin pressed against my hard edges, smoothing me out as she spreads her legs. I pump my shaft hard as I imagine her climbing on top of me, riding me with her creamy pussy.

Damn, I'm gonna come hard, and I can't stop picturing her above me, her tits in my mouth, her body ready to be devoured like a fucking candy box.

My cock explodes as I picture her going down on me, licking my hardness like a lollipop. Her mouth wrapped around my stiff dick, her hands on my tight balls, my come filling her mouth.

Fuck. I close my eyes, knowing I haven't gotten off like that in my whole damn life. No woman has gotten me so hard, so damn fast.

And to think, I wasn't even in bed with Hazel. Only the idea of her.

I fall asleep with her as the only thing on my mind.

In the office the next day, I'm going over the calendar when my sisters, Greta and Maggie, come into the shop. Greta drops off a tray of sticky buns from their bakery, and Maggie places half a dozen cupcakes on the counter.

"You two are my favorite girls in this town, you know that, right?" Charlie says, grabbing a cupcake and tearing off the wrapper. "Oh, God," he groans. "Red velvet is my favorite."

Maggie suppresses a smile but can't seem to resist commenting. "I know," she says, shrugging like that wasn't intentional.

"You're gonna make me gain twenty pounds if you keep dropping this stuff off here," he tells my sisters.

"It's nothing," Maggie says. "Anyway, Greta's cinnamon rolls are a day old."

Greta rolls her eyes. "You're lucky to have me here at all. Milo was up half the night fussing that his favorite blanket was in the wash. I need a nap and it isn't even noon."

My sisters have the only bakery in town. Greta makes the breads, rolls, and loaves. Maggie sticks to cakes, pies, and cupcakes.

"I need a coffee to wash that down." Charlie heads to the back room to get himself a cup, and as he walks away, Maggie watches him with a not-so-discreet sigh.

"Why don't you just ask him out?" Greta asks our younger sister. Greta's the oldest at twenty-eight, then it's me at twenty-seven, and lastly, Maggie's twenty-three. And she's had a thing for Charlie for as long as anyone can remember.

I don't get mixed up in the girl talk. God knows I have nothing to add to that conversation, but I also don't want my little sister with a player like Charlie.

"Yeah, right," Maggie sighs. "He doesn't know I exist. At least, not like that."

I scowl. "Seriously, I don't want to hear any more. Besides, he does know you exist. He's been my best friend since we were ten. He watched you grow up, Maggie." I just shake my head, looking back at the calendar. Girls are so weird sometimes.

"Aren't you gonna ask why we stopped in?" Greta asks.

Maggie teases. "Make him guess."

I raise an eyebrow. "I have no fucking clue."

"You're no fun," Maggie pouts, crossing her arms as Charlie comes back holding a cup of coffee. "We came to tell you that tonight I'm having a party."

"And I care because?"

"Because you need to come," she says. "Milo and Lucy are gone until tomorrow afternoon at Luke's sister's place in Grantsville, so no excuses. Greta's coming and so are you."

"What about me?" Charlie asks, pretending offense.

Maggie swallows. "Of course, you're invited. Everyone is. It's a late-night, backyard BBQ. Everyone's gonna be there."

I snort. "Everyone but me. That sounds about as fun as shopping."

Maggie and Greta frown. "You're no fun, Clive."

Just then the door pushes open and in walks Hazel, holding a small white box in her hand.

"Hey," she says, seeming surprised to see the full office. "Uh, hi, Clive."

"Hey," I say, looking down. The moment I lay eyes on that woman it's like I forget how to mother fucking breathe. She's wearing a white lace dress that comes above her knees, and her hair's pulled back in a braid. Wisps are loose around her face and she has on worn cowboy boots. Looking at her gets me hard, and I step behind the counter, unable to focus. And not wanting her to see what she does to me.

I've been able to stay away from hot women for years, but this one makes me crazy.

Her eyes dart around the office, landing on the counter filled with treats. "Um, well I made you these but, um, looks like you already have plenty." She hands me the white box, looking deflated.

I take them from her, incredibly aware of the fact that my sisters and Charlie are watching us intently.

"No, those are nothing," I say waving off the goods my sisters brought.

"Nothing?" Maggie says butting her head in where it doesn't belong. "Those red velvet cupcakes are not nothing?"

Greta elbows her, and Maggie shuts up. Apparently, the idea of me talking to a woman, without pushing her off after the first word is a revelation.

I meet Hazel's gaze. "My sisters own Two Sisters Bakery in town. They're always shoving food at me."

"Oh." She bites her bottom lip, and damn, she has no idea how fucking sexy she is.

"What is it?" I ask, stepping toward her. Why? I have no goddamn clue, except I have to. I need to be closer to her.

"It's just, um, I made you those... Whiskey gummy bears. I didn't have any guy flavors yesterday and I felt so bad for getting things so wrong." She lifts her chin; our eyes meet and I swear to God I could pull her to me in that instant and never let go.

I have no fucking clue where these instincts come from, but this woman is doing something to me. Something crazy.

"You didn't need to go to all that effort for me."

Her cheeks redden and I'll admit that I like to make her blush. The truth is women in this town have been bringing me homemade lasagnas and apple pies for as long as I can remember to try and win me over, but none of those gestures did anything to my cock.

Hazel though? She makes me fucking ready to go.

"I wanted to," she says softly. "And after realizing I only had treats catering to women, I figured I might as well try my hand at something you might like."

"Thank you," I tell her. "I bet they're delicious."

Hazel licks her lips, and damn, if my sisters and best friend weren't here in my office, I swear to God, I'd fucking groan, pull her little dress up around her waist and give her a real thank you.

I open the box, and Greta and Maggie lean over to look inside. I turn to them. "Do you mind?"

"What?" Greta frowns. "Aren't you even going to introduce us?"

I run my hand over my beard, giving my sisters a hard look, Charlie too. I don't do introductions. I don't do chit-chat. But one look at my sisters and I'm reminded that if I don't take the lead here they will.

Hazel's eyes aren't on me or my sisters. They are taking in the office, and I see her gaze lingering on the photos of Charlie and me all over the office on various outdoor expeditions.

I like that she doesn't feel the need to jump in and be the star of the show. She comes across more reserved, almost shy. And I can tell she felt more at ease when it was just the kids and me yesterday than she is here with my sisters and Charlie. I can't help but wonder why. Who is this woman and why is she here in Linesworth?

Greta taps her fingers on the counter waiting for me to say something but I don't need anyone taking the lead as far as Hazel and I are concerned.

"Hazel owns the new candy cart. The one I took Lucy and Milo to yesterday."

My sister's eyes light up. "You're Hazel! Lucy gave me the gummy roses. One word: divine!"

"Oh, my gosh. We meant to come say hello but Greta had a rush order, and I had a wedding cake."

"It's fine," Hazel says, slowly taking in their energy. There is a lot of it. "I can imagine how busy you must be running a business, with your two kiddos to boot."

"Yeah, not sure what I'd do without Clive," Greta says.

I cough. "Uh, don't you guys need to be somewhere?"

Charlie laughs. "Not really," he says, reaching for a sticky bun. "I work here."

"Yeah, and the kids are with their aunt," Greta says, taking a cupcake. "I'm pretty free."

"And I've got nothing to do except shop for my party." Maggie's eyes gleam. "Oh, my gosh, you should totally come. With Clive." Looking at me she adds, "Don't worry, we only invited half of the local Clive Fan Club."

Hazel's eyes widen. "Um, no, I mean. Thanks but—"

"No, you're new in town," Maggie pushes. "We know nothing about you. And we want to. You have to come. Besides, I've never seen Clive talk to a woman this long, in like, years. So I'm not taking no for an answer."

I press my fingertips to my forehead. My sister is just way too much.

"She said no." I save Hazel from a party I'd never go to without being forced. I avoid them at all cost because they're filled with either happy couples or single women hitting on me.

Hazel looks over at me, and I swear she looks wounded. Dammit, women are so damn complicated.

"Well, I mean, unless you want me to come," Hazel says.

I look around the room. Charlie thinks this is hilarious, and my sisters, they are dying to sink their teeth into this sweetheart who came calling for me.

"Uh, do you want to come?" I run my hand through my hair. When was the last time I asked a woman out?

"Sure." She smiles without showing her teeth, and I know she's holding something back.

My sisters and Charlie finally get a goddamn clue and leave out the front door, apparently satisfied that I won't fuck this up.

"My sisters are bossy, so just be prepared for them tonight," I tell her, reaching for one of the candies she made and popping it into my mouth.

Truth is, I'm not sure where I want this thing to go. I know where I want Hazel; in my bed, but she isn't the sort of girl you can sleep with and forget. She's trouble in a way I don't think she understands.

She tilts her head as if considering me.

"What?" I ask, reaching for another gummy bear.

"Do you like them?" she asks.

"They're fucking delicious."

She smiles softly, tucking a strand of hair behind her ear, looking pretty damn tasty herself.

I clear my throat, trying of think about something besides her long legs and heart-shaped face. "I'll pick you up then?"

"Perfect," she says.

And all I can think is, yes, Hazel. You are indeed.

Chapter 4

HAZEL

The guest house I'm renting sounds fancier than it is, but it is just a block off Main Street, and so the location works perfectly. And on top of that, the studio is clean and quiet. There's a small kitchenette where I can make tea in the morning and a big bathtub where I can take a long soak at night. It is more than enough for me.

Certainly, more than I ever had growing up.

I turn on the shower, wanting to wash some of the sweat and sugar off my skin before my date. Stripping out of my dress and kicking off my boots, I step into the shower, letting the warm water soak me. I close my eyes, thinking through the day.

Sales were good. Better than good, actually. And for only being a few days in business, I can already see how being in a tourist town like this is going to be great. My biggest concern is what I will do when it gets cold or rains. I'll have to close down my cart. There aren't any indoor markets in this village, and that's why I need a shop of my own so badly.

I can't worry about that right now. My entire life can't be about my candy. Making a few friends would be nice. I haven't had the luxury of thinking about friendships for years. Now that I'm here, starting over, I have a chance to be more than a caregiver and provider. Still, a party isn't my first choice. Maybe a dinner with a few ladies, meeting for a drink. A party is not exactly what I'd call my comfort zone.

But I was asked out by a real man. Clive might not be the most outgoing man in the world, but he just might well be the hottest.

His shoulders pulled the tee-shirt he wore today taut and seeing him in his office, where maps hung all over the wall as well as pictures of him on outdoor adventures, I couldn't help but imagine myself being on a forest expedition with him.

As I wash my hair and rub soap over my skin, I lose myself in that idea. Clive's strong hands pushing up my dress, pulling down my panties, his hands holding me tightly and taking me places I've never gone before.

My legs part as my fingers move gently toward my clit, my body hot at the thought of Clive pressing his fingers against me. I gasp as my fingers move faster and faster, dreaming of Clive lifting me at the waist, his pants dropped, his cock under me... inside of me. I moan as I lift a leg up on the side of the tub, my fingers working themselves into a frenzy as I near orgasm.

I take myself to the edge as I imagine him ripping off my dress, burying his face against my breasts, grinding his length inside me. I come, hard. My body tensing as I let the sensation wash over me.

My hand reaches for the water, pushing it all the way to cold. My body is primed and on fire and desperate for more.

I let my skin calm down as ice-cold water rushes over me.

Get yourself together, I think. This is a date. Nothing more.

Heaven knows I've never had more than this before, so why would I think a man as perfect as Clive would be interested in taking my virginity?

———

When Clive arrives at my place, I've calmed down. But I'd be lying if I said I wasn't excited at the prospect of getting to know him better. A lot better. And when he knocks on my door, I remind myself that anything can happen. This is my life after all.

"You look beautiful, Hazel," he tells me, his voice low and gravelly like he's working hard to keep himself together.

For a moment I doubt if he really wants to be there, with me. His sisters did kind of push the issue.

But then he looks me in the eyes and his icy blues tell me everything I need to know.

He wants to be here. With me.

And when he takes my hand in his, leading me to the sidewalk, my body feels electric.

I know he feels it too, because he shakes his head, biting his bottom lip. "Damn, woman, where did you come from?"

"Nowhere good."

He frowns. "I don't believe that. You are the sweetest thing that's ever landed in this town. No way do I believe you've been anywhere that wasn't good."

I twist my lips, not sure I want to unload all of my baggage on him on our first date. "I brought caramel corn. Do you think that's okay?" I pat the tote bag that is slung over my arm.

"That's fine. Though you didn't need to bring anything. It's Maggie's place. I bet she has a whole setup."

"Is she the party planner of the family?" I ask, noticing the looks we're getting as we walk down the street. I swear women left and right are giving us a double take.

"Yeah, she likes to be the center of attention," Clive smirks. "I don't get that vibe from you though."

"I'd say the same about you."

"You picked up on that?" he asks.

I laugh softly. "Um, every woman we've walked past is giving you those eyes and yet you don't give them a second glance."

"What kind of eyes, exactly?"

"Sex crazed." I elbow him playfully. "Don't tell me you don't notice. It was like that yesterday at my cart too. Every woman in this town seems to have their eyes on you."

"Eh, I don't date much."

"Me either," I admit.

We turn right, leaving Main Street and start heading down a neighborhood street. This town is idyllic—just like I remembered. Picket fences and apple trees, tree forts in backyards and kids riding bicycles down sidewalks. It's the kind of dream town that I want to raise a family in, grow old in. The kind of place that feels like forever.

"That's hard to believe," Clive says.

"Likewise." I swallow, not wanting to overshare, knowing that a man like Clive isn't the loud and obnoxious type who would tell anyone else my history but also, I don't want to scare him off.

We walk hand in hand a few more blocks, silently. And when he doesn't offer up additional details about his life, I'm glad I didn't either. In fact, maybe this is a mistake, thinking he's a man who might understand me. Maybe he is just man candy—a sexy guy who will take me to a party—but nothing more.

But then he stops walking and turns to face me.

"Look, Maggie's place is the next house. And I want to prepare you." He clenches his jaw and I have an insane urge to push back the hair on his forehead and pull him close against me. My emotions feel like a rollercoaster when I am next to Clive and I don't think that's the sort of ride for me.

I don't want a rollercoaster romance, I want a carousel. A romance that is safe and steady, but still magical.

"Hazel," he warns me. "People there are gonna talk. They'll want to know why I'm out with you. They're gonna give me a hard time, give us a hard time."

My eyes flash with confusion. "Is there something wrong with me?" I look down. I'm in a sundress and sandals, nothing out of the ordinary. But maybe he doesn't think I'm pretty enough to be with a man as handsome as him.

He shakes his head. "What? No. You're perfect Hazel. You're... hell, you're the reason I'm out at all."

"What do you mean?"

"I haven't gone out in years. I haven't met a woman that interested me enough. But you... I don't know what it is, but you make me forget myself. I've talked to you only a few times but damn woman, you are..." he breaks off.

I inhale, not sure where this is going to go. I lower my chin, but he lifts it, forcing me to look in his eyes.

"Hazel, you are different than the rest. And that is a motherfucking compliment. I hate parties, but I wanted a reason to see you."

I smile then, relief covering me. "You could have just asked me out, you know."

He shrugs. "Well, now we've at least got to show our faces, otherwise, my sisters will hassle me about it for the next month." He leans down, his mouth close enough to kiss. "You don't mind that I'm not a party person?"

A laugh escapes me. "I'm not a party person either. I'm more of a roam the bookstore with a cup of tea person. Or sit around a campfire and look at the stars person."

The look he gives me intensifies, but instead of kissing me, he steps away.

Okay, so that wasn't the right thing to say and I don't know why.

"You're not a reader?" I try.

He runs a hand through his hair. "It's not that."

"Okay." I press my lips together, not understanding this man. One moment he appears so into me. The next he's as cold as the shower I took tonight.

"Hey," he says, squeezing my hand. "Let's go say hello and then get out of here. How does that sound?"

"Together? You still want to spend time with me?" I ask.

"I do, Hazel." He clears his throat. "I get the feeling that hearing that from me is a surprise, and I don't understand why that is."

I exhale, deciding to be brave with him. "When you've had a life like mine you know to keep expectations in check, but at the same time, it feels as if I have turned a page in the story of my life."

"You believe all that after just moving into town?"

I lick my lips. "I feel that way after meeting you."

His hand is on my waist, he pulls me close. "That's the nicest thing anyone has said to me in a long fucking time, Hazel."

I close my eyes, knowing his hand holding me is the sweetest sensation I've ever experienced. His hands, though strong and tough, hold me like I am something fragile, something delicate. It makes me melt against him.

"Maybe it's naïve, Clive," I whisper. "But I choose to believe that this chapter is where my story takes a sharp turn."

"Where will it lead?" he asks, his lips nearing mine, I can taste the kiss that is going to happen. It fills the air and makes me lose myself.

"For the first time in forever, there is a possibility for a happy ending. And I want that ending more than anything."

He groans and presses his lips to mine under the light of the fading sun, against the backdrop of the summer breeze, deep in the heart of the place I want to spend forever.

His kiss is powerful; stirring emotions inside me I didn't know I needed to let out. My body awakens against him, and I know his does too.

Our kiss is too hot for the sidewalk; our kiss belongs in a bedroom, behind closed doors. Our kiss is for our eyes only.

Chapter 5

CLIVE

The woman gets me hard, hot, bothered, and she is dangerous in the most delicious way. I swear to God, I'd pull her behind a bush and take her right here and now, but Greta interrupts a divinely perfect moment.

"Get a room, you crazy kids," she hollers, walking past us with feigned shock. "The children could see."

Hazel steps from me and looks around. "Where are the kids?" she asks.

Greta just laughs. "No kids. They're at my late husband's sister's house tonight. I was just teasing."

Hazel nods, pressing her fingertips to her lips, and I can tell she is visibly flustered.

Good, I like knowing I did that to her. I damn well know she is doing the same exact thing to me.

"Come on you two. Maggie is gonna have a fit if we don't show."

"Understood," I tell her, slipping my hand around Hazel's waist. There's no way in hell I'm letting go of her now.

The three of us walk toward Maggie's house and Greta starts chatting up Hazel. The whole time, the words we exchanged before our kiss are ringing in my ears.

She wants a happy ending.

Damn, it makes me crazy. I want that for her too but I also know it's what my sister wanted. And then her husband Luke died. And there was nothing about that ending other than sorrow.

"So, what brought you to Linesworth?" Greta asks Hazel as we push open the backyard gate to Maggie's house.

"I needed a new start," Hazel says. "And I had a happy memory here as a kid, and I always wanted to return."

"And the candy cart, did you run that before you moved?"

"No, I built it right before I moved over from Seattle."

My sister's eyes go wide. "You built that?"

Hazel laughs. "Well, with the help of the local home improvement store, yes. I am a DIY kind of girl."

"Impressive," Greta says. "I can't even unclog my own toilet without calling for help. Let alone build something."

Hazel smiles softly. "If you don't have anyone to call you kind of have to do it on your own."

Greta's eyes soften, realizing what Hazel is saying. She has no one and I don't know what has happened to get Hazel to where she is right now, but I am more and more grateful she landed here.

"Well, now you're here in Linesworth where everyone helps everyone."

Greta squeezes Hazel's arm before telling her she's gonna go say hi to a few people.

Coming up behind her, I push away her hair, lean in and whisper in her ear. "You okay?"

She turns, and my arms effortlessly wrap around her waist. "With you here, yeah."

And I know I hardly know this woman but it also feels like I've known her forever. Like she fits with me, and I want to know every last thing about her.

I've never been like this before. Never falling head over heart, but Hazel isn't like anyone else.

She is sweet as fuck and breaking through my hard candy shell.

————

An hour later it's time to make our retreat but it's hard to leave because the women Maggie invited are exceptionally forward tonight. It's like seeing me with a date has brought out the competition. And I hate that for me, but especially for Hazel. She doesn't need to deal with this bullshit.

Hazel is just finishing her lemonade when the woman who owns the yoga studio in town grabs my elbow.

"Clive, I've got to talk to you, we're doing the Man Candy Calendar again this year to raise money for the fire department and we wanted to know if you wanted a month."

"That'll be a hard pass," I say, looking over at Hazel who widens her eyes and I know she's got opinions about this. Hell, so do I.

"Oh, Clive, you've got to. Charlie agreed. Maybe you could do a page with him?"

I snort. "You think I'm gonna agree to strip to my tighty-whities alongside my oldest friend? Fat chance."

"Oh, come on, Clive, please," Yoga-lady begs.

Hazel laughs good-naturedly. "It's for a good cause though, Clive," she says, holding back a laugh. "Think of all the money you could raise if you'd take off your shirt."

I shake my head and smirk at my date. She's being so naughty.

"It's not gonna happen," I say with a smile, before grabbing Hazel by the waist and squeezing her to me. "You really want me to strip down for all the women of this town?" I growl in her ear.

She giggles, shaking her head. "I suppose not. However, I wouldn't mind seeing you strip down just for me."

Her words tell me everything I need to know. I need to get my woman out of this party and into a bed. Stat.

"It's time to go, Sugar Plum," I say taking her hand in mine, gripping it tightly, not wanting to waste time on long goodbyes with my sisters.

———

On our way out, I tell Charlie I'll see him tomorrow,

knowing he hardly hears me. He's got some woman I've never seen before hanging on his arm.

Unfortunately, Maggie intercepts Hazel on our way out.

"Did you have fun?" Maggie asks, her white sangria sloshing.

"It was great. Thanks again for the invite," Hazel says.

"I'm so glad. We need to be friends. Especially since you're in the business of sweets, just like me. Oh, did you meet Carla? You have to." She reaches for Hazel's hand.

I raise a brow. "Actually we're gonna go, Maggie." Hazel nods in agreement. Good, she wants out of here too.

"But Hazel has to network," Maggie pushes. "Especially since once the rainy season starts she'll need connections so she can keep selling her stuff in other shops in town."

"Not tonight, she doesn't."

"Fine." Maggie rolls her eyes, knowing not to push me. "But you'll come back, right, Hazel?"

"Totally," Hazel agrees, then, without another word, she reaches for my hand, silently asking me to take her away from the crowds, the inside jokes, and the booze. I noticed she didn't drink anything but club soda for the last hour.

Walking away from the party is easy for both of us it seems, and the knowledge relaxes me for the first time since we stepped foot at Maggie's. I couldn't concentrate on anything besides Hazel and all I wanted to do was kiss her again.

We slowly walk back to her house, and I ask what she thought of the night.

"It was good. Your sisters sure are nice."

I laugh. "Opinionated, bossy, obnoxious. Those are the words I'd use."

"They aren't so bad. Besides, you guys are really lucky to have one another."

"You don't have anyone?"

She shakes her head. "It's fine by me. Everyone I've ever relied on has let me down."

"Which is why you're a DIYer?"

She laughs. "Something like that."

When we get to her house, she takes out her key. "Will you come in?"

I nod. "I live in my sister's guest house. If we went there everyone would know our business."

She nods in understanding and we step inside her small studio space. She shuts the door, locks it too.

"Home sweet home," she says, reaching to turn on a lamp on a side table.

"You just moved in last week, right?"

"Yep." I watch Hazel straighten a throw blanket on the end of her queen-sized bed.

"You got it set up pretty fast."

"I wanted it to feel like home." Hazel smiles. "What does your place look like?"

I explain how there are still unhung pictures, three years later. How I've never bought proper curtains and just have sheets tacked to the windows to keep out the sun.

"You are such a guy."

"This is true." I step toward her, thinking about her lips—our kiss. Needing it again. "But I don't want to be here forever. I'm looking at property, to build a place of my own."

"That sounds wonderful. And you'd build a house all on your own?"

"For the most part. I'd call in guys to help with some of it, but I've worked outside all my life, kind of preparing for this. I moved into Greta's place after Luke died. She had a rough go for quite a while. Needed someone to take Lucy to school and potty-train Milo. She spent a lot of time in bed. Years, practically. And it was an honor to help out. But now the kids are getting older, and I think she's finally in a lot better place."

"She's lucky to have you. To go through hard patches with family supporting you? That's amazing."

"And you?" I ask. "You picture yourself here for a while?"

She tilts her head to the side as if embarrassed. "I'd like to get a place of my own someday, too."

I raise my eyebrows. "Property?"

"Not for a house—for a shop. You know how Maggie mentioned earlier the rainy season? It's been my biggest concern with this business plan. Rain and snow don't work well for outdoor candy carts."

"Makes sense. And there are always a few available storefronts on Main Street."

"I know." Her face brightens, looking up at me.

"And one day, when I save enough, I'll have one of my own."

I push a strand of hair from her eyes. "I like the dreams you have. The fact you moved here, all on your own, starting something out of nothing. A lot of people wouldn't be that brave."

Her eyelids close and I know my words are what she needed to hear tonight.

"It's our one wild and precious life," she whispers. "Mary Oliver wrote that."

My heart just about cracks at those words—they are fucking beautiful—just like Hazel. I can't hold back anymore, and I don't want to.

"I'm going to kiss you now."

"Good," she says. And I cup her face with my hands, and I draw her to me. My mouth presses against hers, her lips are blossom soft and taste like nectar—sweet and subtle and soothing. Her lips don't ravish me. They promise comfort and security. Her lips are not the kind you forget. Her kisses are the sort that stay with a man forever.

Her lips part and my tongue finds hers. She whimpers against me, her body as needy as mine. I pull away from her sugary-sweet lips and look into her eyes. "You want wild and precious?"

She nods, her lips swollen and so fucking beautiful.

"Then tonight, let me give that to you."

Chapter 6

HAZEL

It happens so fast—but I had been waiting for this my entire life. A man who would take his time with my body and show me that I was more than the sum of my past.

And when Clive turns me around and his fingers pull down the zipper on my dress, I take a deep breath, knowing that tonight my body is his. I will open myself up and let my guard down and I won't tiptoe around what I desire.

I will give in, entirely.

The zipper is down and he gently tugs at the straps. In a flash, the dress is on the floor, and I step from my sandals, looking down at myself, trying to see what he will see. I wore a white lace bra and panties, and my tummy isn't exactly flat. My hips aren't either. I make candy for a living, for goodness sakes. But in Clive's arms, I feel small, protected. His broad shoulders make me feel petite and that gives me confidence.

When Clive spins me to face him. It's like he doesn't see my imperfections. He just sees me.

"I've never done this," I tell him. "But I want to. With you. Tonight."

His eyebrows raise, his hand running over his beard. I've learned that it's the gesture he makes when he's thinking something through.

"You're a virgin?"

I nod, hoping it won't change things. Women have been eyeing him all night, so I know he's been with women before. That doesn't bother me. I know none of us can change the past, not that he'd want to. Still, I want this with all that I am.

"Does that make you change your mind?"

His eyes sear into mine.

"I'm not a fragile, breakable thing," I tell him.

He shakes his head, stepping closer and cradling me in his arms. "Oh, Hazel, how wrong you are."

I swallow, thinking he might walk away, leaving me undressed and alone.

I don't want to be alone anymore.

"Being fragile isn't a bad thing. It's a beautiful thing. Being fragile doesn't mean you're not also strong. And I want to be gentle with you, regardless of your past. I told you tonight would be wild, but precious too. You, Hazel, are precious."

I blink back tears, ones I hadn't expected. And then Clive is pulling off his tee-shirt and taking off his jeans and standing before me, ripped and rugged and mine for the taking.

"Oh, God," I mutter.

"Is this where you decide I'm too fragile for you?" he jokes, reaching around my waist, and pulling me close. I feel his hardness through his boxers, and it awakens me to my core.

I bite back a smile. "You are not fragile." I tentatively run my hand over his chiseled chest. "You are solid." I smack his abs, proving all six of them are as firm as they look.

"Oh, baby," he groans. "I'm not just solid. I'm rock hard."

He takes my hand and presses it against his length, and my eyelids flutter, feeling a cock for the first time. He is big and thick and I need to see more. I need it all.

His fingers slip under the waistband of my panties, easing them down. And then my pussy is bare and I need him bare, too. I hook my fingers into his boxers and tug, freeing his cock and seeing exactly what he is made of.

I gasp at the size, the length. He is all man—man candy. And he was made to please. It may be lewd to think, but all I want is to lick his hard lollipop until I get a sugar rush.

He unhooks my bra and tosses it aside. His hands taking hold of my round breasts and he runs his fingers over them, plucking my nipples and shaking his head. "Your tits are fucking insane, Hazel. So perky and perfect." He lowers his head, his tongue licking them, sucking on them.

My hands run through his hair, and with eyes closed, I let the sensation of his mouth against my breasts rush over me. It makes me feel beautiful and alive and when my fingers circle around his cock I forget to breathe.

Catching my breath, I move closer to him, his long, velvety length needy and so is my body.

Clive draws me to the bed and when I'm lying on my back, he spreads my legs. "You are my heaven," he says, his voice hushed, as he kisses my thighs. His lips make love to my pussy and when he dips his tongue inside me, licking me and leaving kisses against my most tender spots, I forget all about what led me to Linesworth. I forget about my mom and sister dying. I forget the man who hurt them, and whom I escaped. I forget the heartache and heartbreak that left me alone, scared, and broken. I had no one but myself. In this moment, I forget all that.

In this moment, I am not alone. Clive is here, taking away my bad memories and replacing them with kisses.

His tongue runs up and down my wet slit, and a finger slips inside me. My knees buckle, wondering if feeling this good is too much, too soon, but then Clive looks up and our eyes meet.

My knees drop, my fear cowed with his solid promise of taking care of me tonight.

"You taste like cherries," he tells me with a smile.

"Don't tease me," I say playfully.

"I would never." He pulls himself up, over me, and his cock is hard against my belly.

"Thank you," I whisper.

He grins, then leaving kisses on my cheek, my collar-bone, right between my breasts. "I haven't earned a thank you yet."

"Then do what it takes to get one, Clive." I arch my back, telling him not to wait any longer.

He reaches for his jeans, and finds a condom. I resist teasing him about expectations. The truth is, when I showered today, I touched myself with visions of his naked body playing in my mind. I had hoped the night would end the exact same way.

He rolls it on his massive cock and my legs open, wrapping around him. I may have never done this before, but my body knows what my mind doesn't.

"You feel so goddamn good," he tells me.

"You haven't even tried to go inside," I say with a half-smile.

He shakes his head, his hand on his cock guiding himself toward me. "No, under me. Next to me. With me. That's what feels good, Hazel. That is what feels so damn right."

Then he presses himself inside me, ever so slowly, taking what is mine as I offer what I want him to have.

"Am I hurting you?" he asks, his hands pushing back the hair on my forehead, his other arm holding him up on my side so his powerful body doesn't crush me.

"Not in a way that's unbearable," I tell him truthfully.

"The pain will pass," he promises.

"It always does," I say, my voice hitching at the truth. My eyes close as he enters me more fully. My pussy screams for just a moment as Clive's words become true. With his cock inside me, the pain turns to pleasure. The hurt becomes hope. And our bodies collide with a crash.

"Clive," I whimper, my legs wrapping around him, wanting to be closer until we are one. I don't know what's happening to my heart, but it's being stripped of things I pretended I no longer harbored deep inside. The wounds of my past heal as Clive moves against me, ever so slowly.

Not all men are here to kill and destroy.

Some men are here to have and to hold.

So, I'll hold on tight and won't let go.

I don't know what will happen tomorrow with Clive and me but I know that right now, he is giving me a gift.

He rocks against me, my body opening to his.

Our fingers lace; our bodies one, as we come together.

And when we come, it's more than wild and precious.

It's a miracle in the making.

Chapter 7
CLIVE

Her body moves against me all night long. We find a rhythm as we move as one. On her knees, she takes my cock, sucking me with a smile splayed on her angel face. I come against her, and she swallows me, wiping her mouth and telling me I'm whipped cream and sprinkles.

I already had the cherry on top when she gave me her virginity.

I lick her cunt until she drips and my beard is coated in her desire and damn, her pussy is the sweetest thing I've ever tasted. Which is saying something, because her lips are candy in and of themselves.

When we are spent in every way, and then some, I hold her close and ask her what brought her here, why she has no one else.

"It's not a pretty story."

I cradle her in my arms, looking deep into her eyes. "I don't want a pretty story. I want your story."

"I don't want to scare you away, Clive." Her voice is

so soft it's a whisper. "Whenever I talk about it, I start crying."

I pull her closer. "I promise to be here, ready to wipe your tears away."

My promise soothes her, and she begins to open up, one memory at a time, revealing a life that is heart-breaking and brave. Hazel is a survivor, and she is that much more beautiful because of it.

She tells me her stepfather was a nightmare, but that he got locked up two years ago for murdering her family. The truth shocks me, and I ask how the hell she moves on from that sort of pain, how she smiles and makes candy for a living when she has been through so much. How does one swallow something that bitter and come out so damn sweet?

She rests her head against my chest, telling me that if she forfeited living her best life, then her step-dad would have another victim. Her. And she wasn't going to lose her life because he took the lives of the people she loved.

I thought Hazel was a gift before... but her words tell me she is more than that. She is a golden treasure. How anyone can be so strong in the face of tragedy amazes me. She is more than I deserve.

I kiss her, not wanting her dreams to be clouded by those bad memories. I kiss her, wanting her to drift away feeling safe.

When we fall asleep, our bodies are a tangle of sweat and sex and something more.

Something that wakes me dead in the night.

Something that fucking terrifies me.

Hazel has already lost so damn much. My biggest fear has always been dying while on the mountain just like Luke. Leaving the person I loved, someone who can't pick up the pieces on her own, just like my sister.

I can't do that to Hazel. That's why I swore off women in the first place. I won't be the reason Hazel experiences any more pain. She, more than anyone I have ever met, deserves to be happy.

And falling in love? It's just too damn risky.

Watching my sister lose Luke was hell.

And if she hadn't fallen in love with him, she wouldn't have spent three years putting herself back together.

She would have always been whole.

And I won't do that to Hazel. It's better to walk away before either of us falls in too deep.

I slip out of the bed and find my clothes. I kiss her cheek, pull the blanket up around her shoulders and silently tell her goodbye.

————

After going to my place and packing a backpack with a week's worth of supplies, I email Charlie, not telling him anything other than I'd be gone for a week on a solo trip. I'm not ready to get all touchy-feely with him—especially when it comes to Hazel.

I begin a hike straight out of town knowing it's less than five miles to the national forest anyway. As the night turns to dawn, I begin my ascent into the mountains, not looking back.

Chapter 8
HAZEL

When I wake to an empty house, I tell myself Clive went out for coffee. After thirty minutes pass, I decide he must have had to leave early for work. I look on my kitchen table, thinking maybe he left a note—but there's nothing.

Deciding that there must be an explanation I don't understand, I decide to shower and get my day going regardless. It's Sunday and a busy day in town, or so I've heard. And I need to get out there and hustle my candy if I want this business to succeed.

I look at my bed longingly, remembering how Clive and I rolled around in it for hours last night.

My legs are sore but my heart is full. And even when I step in the shower and lather up with soap, I can't wash the smile off my face.

People say you can't fall in love at first sight and maybe that is true. But I think you can fall in love after one date because that is what I think is happening to me.

It's not lust or infatuation. Clive may be sexy as hell, but he is so much more than meets the eye. His rough exterior that drives women wild is not for show. He keeps parts of himself hidden to protect whatever he has buried, and if I had the privilege of helping him shake off some of that armor, it would be an honor.

I want to know him, all of him. And I want him to know all of me. Because when Clive looks in my eyes, it's like he sees me as the best version of myself, and I want to be that woman for him.

So, as I dress for the day and slide lip-gloss on and pull my hair into a bun on the top of my head, I think about stopping by his office and letting him know I how I feel. Not all of it at once, of course. But I want him to know that for me, I see real potential between us.

After steering my cart from my guest house garage, I walk the block into the village square and then I park it without setting up the awning. First I want to stop in and tell Clive that next time he needs to leave a note.

Pushing open the door to Forest Expeditions, I see Charlie sipping from a cup of coffee.

"Hey Charlie," I say. "Have you seen Clive?"

He sets down his coffee and shrugs. "No, it was weird, actually. He emailed me saying he was going on a solo trip this morning. I honestly thought he must be taking you somewhere."

I frown. "Where did he go?"

"Not sure. You know Clive, he is a man of few words."

I think back to our night, how open and vulnerable we were with one another. Sure, he may be standoffish around other people, but with me, his heart seemed wide open.

"Right. Well, okay then." I feel deflated. Rejected. Alone. Those aren't emotions I ever thought I'd feel when it came to Clive.

Charlie shakes his head. "Didn't you leave Maggie's party together?"

"Yeah, he stayed the night."

Charlie's eyes widen. "No shit."

I twist my lips together. "What's that supposed to mean?"

"Clive doesn't do that. Ever. Not since Luke died." He must sense my discomfort. "No, Hazel, it's good. It's great. He's so damn reserved all the time, it's just..."

"Just what?" I ask, my heart beating fast.

"It's just... you know, him leaving right after... It's a little..."

"Sketchy?" I say, swallowing my tears.

Charlie pats my arm. "No one is better in the woods than Clive. I mean, no one better than me, of course," he says with a lopsided grin. "But he can take care of himself out there. You don't need to worry."

I thank him and ask him to tell me if he hears anything.

As I walk away, all I can think is that sure, Clive can take care of himself in the woods. I don't doubt that.

But I want to help take care of him here.

And by the looks of things, he doesn't feel the same way.

Chapter 9

CLIVE

I've done this trip a thousand times. Camped out at night, hiked to the top of Mount Ellen in day one. The hike is a beaut. There are fifteen pitches of exposed, often knife-edge 5.9 alpine climbing. It's a gorgeous peak and earned a spot in the Fifty Classic Climbs of North America.

After that, I continue on into the Cascade Range, taking in the mountain air, crisp with lingering snow and ice, and the chill in the late summer air tells me the winter is gonna be rough. I sleep in my one-man tent, and then wake up and build a campfire, drinking dark coffee and eating oatmeal, trying my damnedest to forget Hazel.

Hazel, with her hand-stitched apron and her home-made everything. She isn't just sweet—she has true grit. The kind of woman who could handle a man like me. Hell, she's practically tamed me after only a few days.

That's why I knew I needed to walk away. It is too dangerous to love like that. So completely.

Because when you lose that sort of love—life no longer holds any meaning. How could I wake up and face the day if I lost Hazel?

So, I am saving us both from ourselves.

I'm sure she woke up that morning, alone in her bed, angry as hell at me.

But in time, she will be better for it.

As I begin the climb of South Ridge, I know that navigating the serac wall several hundred feet to the right from its apex, over the north face will require some WI4 ice climbing. It's my favorite part of this entire range. I need to summit this ridge in order to descend the north side, where the terrain is easier to traverse.

But instead of thinking about my fucking climb—I'm thinking about Hazel, wondering if she'd like to come up here with me someday. I should be forcing her from my mind, but instead, I'm imagining the bright sun shining on her face, how beautiful she'd look up her with a backdrop of white, snow-covered mountains.

And that's when my feet slip once. Twice.

This is not going to work. I move as slowly as I can, attempting to get passed the unforgiving slope, but my body isn't as small as it needs to be to pass this unscathed. I take a leap, knowing I'm stuck right here forever otherwise. There's no wiggle room on this edge.

Shit. Shit. Motherfucking shit.

I fall.

Fucking hard.

The tumble is more than a drop.

It's a goddamn crash.

I feel my satellite phone crunch beneath me, in my pack. My fucking lifeline was gone.

My body hits an icy patch, my head slams against a rock.

My eyes see vicious bright white lights.

Our one wild and precious life.

Black tunnels block my sight.

There is nothing.

Nothing.

I am gone.

Chapter 10
HAZEL

There are no guarantees to a happily ever after.

And maybe I was a fool to think I'd find mine the first week I moved to a new town.

But after Clive has been gone for five days, I'm not so foolish anymore.

I can be brave and strong.

I need a man who is here for me, one who doesn't run and hide.

But then the rain starts falling.

Hard.

And I all by myself, I push my cart, the one I made by hand, nail by nail, stitch by stitch, under an awning, wishing that I didn't just have my bootstraps to hold onto.

I'm tired of doing it all on my own.

Maggie and Greta run from their bakery, coming to help get my cart under cover, and I'm grateful that they are here and can help, but it is like pouring salt on a wound.

They have one another. They aren't in any of this alone.

And they have Clive.

And me? I have nothing.

I have never been a pessimist; never thrown a pity-party even once in my life. But right now? Right now, I feel like, with one wrong word, I could become a puddle just like the ones filling the village square.

"Sweetie, it's gonna be okay," Greta says, patting my back as I wipe tears from my eyes. They think it's just the cart, the rain—but it is so much more.

I was ready to give their brother everything.

All of me.

I already gave him my body but that isn't all. I wanted to give him my heart. My soul. My forever.

I'm not crazy. I just fell in love with a man the first week we met.

I wipe my eyes, not wanting them to see me this way. Small and weak and alone.

"Why don't you come to the bakery and get some coffee and a cinnamon roll," Maggie says.

"Yeah," Greta agrees. "The cart will be fine, it's right outside our window."

Knowing no one's going to buy candy from an outdoor cart in this wet weather, I let them lead me inside.

A few minutes later, I've dried myself off with hand towels, and am sitting with a warm cup of coffee and a piping hot cinnamon roll.

"So, Charlie says you stopped by the office..." Greta starts.

I swallow, regretting telling Charlie that Clive had spent the night. But I'm sure they all know that now so there is no point in pretending otherwise.

"You know, the fact that Clive stayed with you is pretty remarkable," Maggie says gently, more gently than I've ever heard her speak. She's usually loud and seems to be overcompensating for something, which makes no sense since she's drop-dead gorgeous, hilarious, and has loads of friends considering how many people were at her party.

"Well, staying with me didn't seem to matter much, to be honest. He left in the middle of the night without an explanation." I press my fingertips to my forehead, feeling so stupid. So blind.

"There is an explanation, actually," Greta says. She looks around the bakery and seeing it is empty, she talks candidly. "After my husband, Luke died, Clive changed. Charlie did too for that matter. See, all three of them were best friends, opened the business together and everything. Luke died while the three of them were on a rafting trip. He drowned and the guys were with him, trying to save him." Greta blinks away her tears, and Maggie reaches over and squeezes her sister's hand.

"After Luke passed," Maggie says, "the guys were never the same. Charlie became a player—sleeping with anything with a pulse, but not opening up to anyone in a real way."

"And Clive," Greta says, "he shut himself off to the possibility of love. He says he'd never want a woman he loved to go through what happened to me after I lost Luke."

When I look into Greta's eyes, it's obvious what happened to her after Luke was gone. She had lost half her heart.

"I understand what Clive is thinking," Greta continues. "He thinks he can protect people by keeping them at arm's length, but that's more painful for everyone."

"I've been through loss, too," I tell the women. "And I am so sorry about Luke." I sigh. "But I don't want to beg a man to decide I'm worth changing for. I want a man who believes that without me saying a word."

Maggie laughs a little too sharply. "I totally understand that." Her face strains, hurting, and I can see she's longing to find her happily ever after, too.

"Clive will come back," Greta says. "Give him another chance when he does."

"He might not want another chance," I say picking up my fork.

"True," Greta says, cocking her head, and looking at me the way my sister used to do when we were little girls. Like she knows something I don't. "But what if he does?"

Chapter 11

CLIVE

When I finally come to, I fear the worst. Blood soaks my clothes, but I know head wounds bleed the worst. And I also know I need to get the fuck off this mountain.

I know I've broken a few ribs. There's a gash on my leg and my vision is blurred, but as I lie on that sheet of ice, I can finally see the fucking light.

I'm not just a man—I'm a goddamned fool and I need to get home.

I need to see Hazel.

I need to set things right.

But as I try to stand my legs give out. I'm forced to crawl, and as I begin to make my way back down the treacherous mountain on all fours, I realize I needed to drop to my knees in order to understand.

Eventually, I'm able to stand, I couldn't have made it down in one piece any other way. It takes days, days where it rains cats and dogs, and I don't see a soul the entire time. I'm moving closer to the valley inch by inch because no one else is stupid enough to be out on this ridge in this weather.

And maybe it's for the best—to be forced to this place in such a desperate way.

My body had to be bruised, broken, and covered in ice in order to thaw.

Now I know what matters. It took nearly cracking my skull to get my head on straight.

I know what I want.

What I need.

But I also know Hazel may not want the same thing. Not after what I've done.

———

When I get to the bottom of the mountain, in my car, I open my glove box and turn on my cell phone. There's no way I can drive myself to a hospital—and that's where I fucking need to go.

Charlie needs to be the one to see me at my worst because I have a few things I need to say to him before I say anything to anyone else.

Charlie finds me, propped against my truck, at the base of the mountain in record time. He must have sped the entire way here, after he got my SOS text.

"What the fuck, man? You need to get to a hospital."

I nod, knowing he's right, and he drives me to urgent care after helping me get in the passenger seat of his truck.

I explain what happened, how I fell and nearly died.

Charlie parks the truck and faces me. "You're

fucking crazy going up there alone. Were you on a death mission?"

I run my hand over my beard, knowing it was a fool's errand, thinking I could run from my feelings. Run from Hazel.

"Losing Luke fucked us up real bad, Charlie," I tell him. "We're being idiots, both of us, in our own ways. It's like living in two extremes, thinking that either way is going to save us from heartache."

"I thought I got a girl pregnant last month," he tells me, shaking his head. "I fucking didn't even remember her when she called me, freaking out. She got her period the next day but damn, even that didn't teach me a lesson."

I don't judge him, but I also know neither of us has dealt with losing Luke in a way that honors his life.

"We can do better. Be better men."

Charlie nods. "You love her?"

I squeeze my eyes, fucking being in a truck with my best friend. Broken ribs protecting my own fragile heart.

"I do," I tell him.

"Your sisters say she's upset, like, real bad. You hurt her man."

"I know." It's so fucking hard to hear that, knowing it's the goddamn truth. "But I think I can make it up to her."

"You better not pull any stops if she's the one."

"You don't think it's crazy, to fall so hard, so fast?"

Charlie just shakes his head, shoving his keys in his pocket. "I don't think falling hard is crazy. I think walking away is the part that was fucking insane."

Chapter 12

HAZEL

I hear from people in town that Clive's home, that he had an accident on the mountain but that he's okay.

I'm not going to be the one to chase him down. I'm not going to make his special candy and smile all sweet.

No.

If he wants me he knows where to find me. At my nearly-falling-apart candy cart. It rained for three days straight and while I think my DIY skills are decent, the elements have their own thoughts on the matter.

The afternoon after Clive has supposedly returned, Greta and Maggie come out to my cart with Lucy and Milo.

"I brought you some flowers," Lucy says offering me a bouquet. "Pink roses are your favorite, right?"

I bring them to my nose and inhale. "They are. Where did you get them?"

"Uncle Clive."

I smile, even though hearing his name hurts a little. "He grows roses?"

Lucy and Milo laugh. "No, silly. He has lots of them though."

Not understanding, I look at Greta and Maggie for an explanation.

"I think you should just come with the kids," Maggie says. "It'll make more sense that way."

I look at my cart, not wanting to leave it unattended.

"We'll stay here and look after it." Greta takes the bouquet from me and smiles eagerly.

Lucy takes my hand, and Milo takes the other. Not wanting to argue with the people who have been so kind to me, I let the kids lead the way.

"Where are we headed?" I ask as they take me down Main Street, passed the bakery and Clive's office. They stop and point to the building across the street.

"You're supposed to go there now," Lucy says.

"Are you coming with me?"

"Nope, we're not allowed."

"I'll hold your hand when we cross the street," I say, thinking that's what they mean.

"Nope, Mama told us we couldn't, no matter what you say."

I laugh in confusion. "Okay, and what is it that I'm looking for across the street?"

"You'll know when you see it." Lucy grins.

"Alright," I say, letting go of their hands, and I wait, watching them walk back toward their mom.

Satisfied that they are safe, I cross the street, not knowing what I'll find.

But when I get closer, I see a trail of pink rose petals on the clean city sidewalk. I cover my mouth, not knowing what to expect. But my heart starts beating faster and faster and I step closer to the building and see it's an empty storefront.

Except it isn't empty.

There is a sign in the window: OPENING SOON: Sweet Dreams.

Tears flood my face because beyond the sign, inside the shop, the trail of rose petals ends at the feet of the man I gave my heart to after just one night.

Pink roses are everywhere. Vases and vases and vases of them. So many I could never count them all. And the store is bright white and empty and I look around, not knowing what to think or feel—but my heart is bursting at the seams.

"Hazel," Clive says, a bandage around his head. "Welcome to Sweet Dreams."

I cover my mouth—not wanting to say something that will break this spell. The one he cast over me the moment we met.

"This is for you. No strings attached. I bought the building outright and put it in your name. It's yours."

"Why?" I ask, my hands now pressed to my heart, scared he doesn't want what I want.

Him. Me. Us.

"Why no strings?" I ask.

His eyes flash a dark blue. "I got scared and ran. And you deserve more than that. I don't want you to think you owe me anything by accepting this gift."

"But you came back," I say. "Does that mean you don't want to stay away?"

He steps toward me and I step toward him.

"That isn't what I mean at all. After Luke died, I swore I'd never fall in love. Because I didn't want anyone to hurt the way my sister hurt. But I almost died up on the mountain, Hazel. And do you know what I realized when I was up there, thinking it was my end?"

I wipe away my tears, unable to imagine losing Clive forever before I ever really had him.

"What did you think?" I ask.

"I realized I was a fool. Life without doggedly pursuing everything we want is barely a life at all. And this is it; this is all we get. Our one wild and precious life."

He reaches for my hands. "Hazel, this is your life too. But I can't wait another day to say this, because the truth is, there are no guarantees. And I know it's fast, and I know it's soon. But I love you. I know that now. And the truth is, I knew that the moment I laid eyes on your sweet face."

My hands tremble, my legs wobble, my heart shaking—unable to contain his words, words that promise, words that have power. Words that offer me everything I've ever dreamed of finding.

Clive cups my cheek with his hand. "I got all these roses, more than we could count because I don't know how much time we have. If there are a dozen days, or dozen years, or more. But if I only had one rose to give, I'd give it to you. And if I had a thousand, I'd give you those, too."

Then Clive drops to one knee and pulls out a black box. He opens it and offers it to me.

"Marry me, Hazel. Be my bride. Let me love you fearlessly. Let me love you forever."

I nod, shaking, falling into him. His arms catching me and holding me.

Like I am something precious.

Like I am his.

He slips the ring on my finger. A simple gold band with a beautiful diamond in the center. But I can't focus on the ring. My eyes, they are locked on his.

I moved to this town hoping to start a new chapter of my life but never expected to have my entire love story written in a week.

Epilogue
ONE YEAR LATER: CLIVE

I pull my wife against me, her blossoming baby belly turning me on.

"Love, you are driving me wild," I tell her, my fingers between her thighs. She is slick with desire, and I pull my finger to my mouth, tasting her. "So damn delicious," I groan.

Her hand runs over my shaft, pumping me up and down, getting me nice and hard.

"I think it's against health codes to fuck in a candy shop," she tells me.

I laugh. "Oh baby, we're not fucking, we're making love."

She showers the air with giggles. We're in the back room, after hours, and I'm helping her clean up shop but I think we're about to make a mess.

As I lift her to the prep counter, I spread her legs, my pants already dropped to the floor.

She leans back, knocking over a bag of powdered

sugar. The billowing white clouds make the air smell sweet.

"You're so naughty," she teases.

"You love it," I say, pulling her ass to the edge of the counter, her pussy is so ready for my cock.

I fill her up, and she bites her bottom lip as she sinks down on me. Her cunt so warm and tight, and I can't believe this tasty treat is my wife.

The mother of my baby.

"Greta says she got hornier the further along she got in both of her pregnancies," Hazel says, her arms wrapped around my neck. Her full tits so fucking hot as I fuck her—er, make love to her.

I cock an eyebrow. "We're not talking about my sister right now."

Hazel bounces on me, and she moans in my ear. "I can't wait to fuck you in our cabin tonight."

I grin, squeezing her round ass. "Oh yeah, baby, why will that be different than right now?"

She laughs, her back arching as she rides the orgasm filling her perfect cunt up.

"Because," she whimpers, "up there we don't have any neighbors for miles and miles." She gasps, her nails digging into my skin as she comes hard. "And here," she sighs. "Here, I have to be quiet because people will hear."

I grin, my cock buried deep inside her, ready to explode. I don't tell her what I already believe to be true. Everyone on the block can hear us if they want to listen. We aren't exactly discreet considering after I help her close up the shop most days, we leave with her hair tousled, chocolate sauce on our cheeks or sugar on our clothes.

I come, and she wraps her arms tighter around me, our baby growing in her belly, between us.

"I love you, Clive," she whispers, holding onto me for dear life.

"I love you more, Hazel." I kiss her nectar-flavored lips, always craving more of her.

When we walk out front, she locks up the shop. A woman tourist looks my way, and licks her lips unabashedly.

But Hazel sees the woman and grins, confident in our love. Leaning into me she says, "Too bad for her, I'm not sharing my man candy."

"Good," I say, squeezing her ass. "Because you're the only woman who can satisfy my cravings."

There are more stories in this series, all set in Linesworth!
Visit Amazon to discover them all!

Mountain Man Cake
Mountain Man Bun
Hashtagged by the Mountain Man
Swiped Right by the Mountain Man
Sugar Mountain Christmas Bride
Sugar Mountain Books 1-3

Chapter One: Charlie

Oktoberfest in a Bavarian-themed village is always a little crazy. This year it's no different. We've been bar hopping all night, celebrating the end of the week's

"What? That they're hot? Willing? Ready?" I laugh, but Hazel doesn't join in.

"I mean, aren't you ready to stop being the local man cake and start being..."

"What?"

"I don't know," Hazel says her voice loud over the noisy crowd. "But don't you just get bored taking home a different girl every night? Don't you ever want more?"

Clive comes back with the drinks and hands me a beer. It's a dark amber, and I take a pull to avoid Hazel's uptight questions.

Running a hand over my beard I cock a brow at Clive. "You gotta rein your woman in, she's giving me shit."

Clive reaches around Hazel's waist, pulling her to him. They look at one another and it's so damn sweet that it makes my teeth hurt.

"Good," Clive says, squeezing Hazel's ass. "She can give you all the shit she wants."

I laugh. "So, you're just gonna let her ride my ass?"

Just then Clive's sisters Maggie and Greta roll up to us carrying shots in both hands.

"Someone says they need a ride?" Maggie asks, always wanting the 411.

"Nobody's going anywhere," Clive says laughing.

Maggie shrugs, giving everyone warm smiles--always the life of the party. "Beer?" She hands one to her brother, and Greta gives one to me, Hazel has her sparkling water. We raise our steins, shouting, 'Cheers' before throwing them back.

"Damn," I say, finishing my beer and setting it down

on the high table beside us. "I haven't seen you drink shots since high school, Greta." Back in the day, all of us felt invincible. Greta and Luke seemed like they had life all figured out--young and in love. And then he died, and everything changed.

She shrugs and then adjusts her little black dress. "I'm getting drunk tonight. I'm bored. And lonely. And have a babysitter."

I look over at Clive, brows raised. Uptight, perpetually tired Greta getting wasted? This I gotta see.

Maggie elbows her sister. "You're not supposed to lead with that. If you want to get laid tonight the last thing you're supposed to do is tell everyone."

"Not true," I say. "It usually works for me."

Greta laughs but Maggie scowls.

"And since when did you become the expert on hook-ups, Mags?" I tease. "I don't think I've seen you out with a guy since you moved back after college."

She frowns, picking up her stein and muttering under her breath, "Not by choice."

I look at her for a beat longer than normal, thinking she looks so hot in her skinny jeans and with her hair piled up on the top of her head. Maggie is way too cute to be single. This girl is so funny, always up for anything, and is usually the one who makes sure everyone is having a good time.

She is also my best friend's little sister and way too much of a sweetheart for a piece of man cake like me.

Greta laughs and my attention turns back to her. And off her little sis. "Thankfully, I'm looking for an older man tonight, Charlie. Thanks, though, for the offer."

I forgot I offered her anything, my mind was on Maggie, but I play along.

"You won't let me work for it?" I tease, knowing damn well Greta is like a bossy older sister and I'd never take that woman to bed. Not when this bar is teeming with options.

Still, Clive takes notice of my words because he adds, "Don't you even think about it, Charlie. My sisters are off-limits. You hear me?"

Greta laughs, but Maggie stays silent, just watching the conversation unfold.

"Oh, don't you worry," Greta says. "I may be ready to start dating again, but you can be guaranteed that it won't be with Charlie. I think I'd catch something."

We all laugh at my expense--and if I were intense I'd let them know that I've been tested and am clean. Being a manwhore doesn't mean I don't know how to fucking use protection.

"I swear, can you even imagine?" Greta continues, driving home the point that she'd never sleep with me. "Luke would roll over in his grave if he got wind of that."

Her words were meant to be light, but they still take the wind out of all of us. The memory of Luke, her husband who died five years ago, was not just any ordinary man. He was special and died in an accident on the mountain way too young.

"Sorry," she mumbles. "I didn't mean to get things so ..."

"Greta, don't apologize," I say, waving over a bartender who is carrying a bottle of Jager around for refills. "Luke was a good man, the best. Let's drink to that. And also, let's drink to you getting wasted!"

We all take up our shot glasses and throw them back.

The alcohol burns my throat, and I catch Maggie's eyes. She mouths a thank you, and I know what it's for. She hates to see her sister upset, she's always looking out for everyone else.

Maggie always has the right words to cheer her sister up, and tonight is no exception. "You need to dance! Come on Hazel, let's get her on the dance floor before she starts throwing herself at men in the bar."

Greta laughs, grabbing Hazel's hand and dragging her along.

Over the last few months, since Clive and Hazel got hitched, the dynamic between Maggie and me has changed. She's become more obvious that her crush on me never faded and for the first time in forever, I am seeing her as a woman.

A woman I want to get to know better.

Hell, Clive and Hazel getting hitched changed me, too. Hook-ups used to be enough for me, a way to numb myself from the pain of losing one of my best friends … but now?

Now I want more.

Thing is… Maggie is Maggie.

My best friend's little sister.

And right now, we're all standing around in a drunken pavilion with plans to party.

Maggie has a knack for turning things around and I

know I was grateful she was able to recover Oktoberfest for all of us. The girls run off, leaving Clive and me to our own devices.

For the next ten minutes, Clive and I talk through the tours we have lined up over the next week. We co-own Outdoor Expedition Tour company and it sounds like I'll be taking a group of men on a three-day hike and then Clive is taking a few father-son duos up the week after.

After talking shop, our eyes wander back to the girls on the dance floor. I can't help but notice the way Maggie smiles at everyone around her. She's laughing with an older woman as if they're long lost friends, and then a second later a group from the local CrossFit gym is shooting the shit with her. I swear she knows everyone in this town.

And while everyone knows her for being so freaking friendly, they know me for being an easy fuck.

Not knowing why I'm so focused on Maggie tonight, I turn my attention to her older sister.

"You think that Greta's really ready to get back in the saddle?" I ask, worried for the mother of two.

Clive shrugs. "I dunno, I guess it makes sense she wants to meet someone. It's been a long time."

We finish our beers, and even with the shots and the loud bar, the night isn't exactly upbeat. Clive seems to want to drive this point home.

"What about you though, Charlie, ever think about changing your ways? It's been a long time since Luke died."

"You're saying it's time for me to stop this bender?" I

ask, giving him a sidelong look. I'd be offended, but we've known one another forever.

Just then the lederhosen-clad college women come up to us, asking if we want to take some shots off them.

Clive lifts his ring finger and flashes them his wedding band, so damn proud. They just smile, oohing and ahhing, and then respectfully turn their attention to me.

"What do you say, mountain man?" the girl with bright red lips asks, slurring her words. Her tits are pushed high, and she's drunk as fuck.

I look over at Clive, whose eyes are on the dance floor watching his woman. Greta is dancing with an old dude and Maggie is making sure everybody's taken care of. She delivers her big sister another beer, then leads them all toward a better corner of the dance floor with fewer people. She's always making sure everyone's having a good time.

Well, almost everyone. I watch a man starts grinding against her on the dance floor, she scowls at him and turns the other way.

Which is crazy-- she's pretty--in that girl-next-door kinda way. She isn't like these women offering me body shots, big tits, and round asses. Maggie is more subdued. Think dark denim and cable knit sweaters--not mini-dresses and hair extensions.

The leader-lady grabs my chin, forcing me to look at her.

"You know they say about men with beards?" the drunk girl asks.

"Oh yeah, what's that?" I say, taking her bait. If I run

over to Maggie right now and pull her close, Clive won't be pleased. If I want to make a move with Maggie--and I do--it's going to have to be without her brother's watchful eyes.

"With a face of fur, you'll make her purr," she says, her words lost to a high-pitched laugh.

Usually, that would be all it would take for me to take her by the waist and pull her in for a kiss. Then I'd take her by the hand and lead her home.

But damn, maybe it's the fact that she so drunk, or the fact that Hazel and Clive have not so gently let me know they think it's time I man up.

Everything seems off tonight. I would never have thought that Greta would be ready to move on, but she's on the dance floor with a guy who's giving her all kinds of attention.

If she can move on, maybe I can too.

Maybe being the local man cake is only fun for so long.

Maybe at some point, it's time to be more than a slice of something sweet.

Maybe I can have my cake and eat it, too.

Chapter 2: Maggie

"Just go talk to him," Hazel says.

I shake my head. "He hasn't been interested in sixteen years. I don't think he's interested now." I look over at Charlie. He's standing with Clive, but a whole group of barely-legal women is hanging all over him. Nothing new, Charlie is the man cake in this town and every warm-blooded woman wants a bite.

Myself included.

"I'm not saying go throw yourself at him. Just maybe, you know, tell him you want to have his babies and make sweet love to him for the rest of your life."

I go bright red; I feel it. The heat rising to my cheeks. "Hazel! You are so bad, you know that right?"

"I know," she says twisting her lips in a smile. Leaning in, she says, "But you've saved yourself, all these years for him. Maybe he ought to know that."

I snort. "Yeah right. That would scare Charlie off for life." We're standing at the bar, getting another shot for me and water for her. "Why did I tell you I still had my V card, anyway?"

Hazel laughs, then pinches my cheeks like we've been best friends forever. I certainly lucked out in the sister-in-law department. Hazel married into our family seamlessly. It was like we'd been waiting for her to arrive all our lives and just never knew it.

And she is so great with Greta's kids, I know Hazel will make a great mom too.

Me though? Motherhood is way off on the horizon. First, I'd like to get laid, then get a husband, a house, picket fence--the whole nine yards. Then, eventually children.

Of course, Charlie doesn't know that he's part of my life plan yet.

We look across the dance floor and see Greta

awkwardly shaking her thang on the dance floor with a man twice her age.

I'd be judging her right now except, damn, she looks smoking hot. And she's having fun. When is the last time she's had any fun that didn't involve My Little Ponies or the Trolls movie?

It makes me want to be braver, too. If my sister, who is a widow, can start to believe in finding love again, why can't I? Watching her out there, dancing with abandon, causes me to break out in a smile. She looks so happy.

And I want some of that for myself.

Hazel starts up again. "I could just casually mention something to Clive about how you and Charlie would make a good coup –"

I cut Hazel off.

"He knows I have a crush on Charlie. This whole town does. The only person who doesn't seem to get it is Charlie himself. And if by some miracle Charlie changes his tune, Clive won't like it. I remember how long it took him to get over Luke and Greta getting together."

Hazel pushes down the lime in her glass, her lips pursed together, considering what I just said.

"Yeah, the alternative is dying an old maid."

I elbow her playfully. "Gosh, Hazel. I'm twenty-three. Lay off!" I laugh it off, even if her teasing does sting a bit. Hazel swooped into this town and fell madly in love in like, a week flat. All it took was a near-death experience and they got the HEA.

Me? I've known Charlie since I was eight years old and the closest physical contact we've made was when he used to give me noogies in junior high. I hated how much I looked forward to those.

"Sorry, babe," she says. "I was just playing. The truth is you deserve a man who realizes how amazing you are." She turns back to the bar to order something and I let my body sway with the crowd around me. I

t is so busy here in Linesworth this time of year, and it's fun to change the pace a bit. And I bet all these tourists will have horrible hangovers tomorrow, which will bode well for our shop, the Two Sister's Bakery. Greta and I will be selling coffee and donuts at the crack of dawn.

Which will be here soon enough. We might as well enjoy the night while it's here.

"Hazel," I call out. "Let's just go dance." I want to have a good time with my sister and our pregnant sister-in-law. And I want to stop thinking about Charlie and the life with him I'll never have.

"Perfect." Hazel returns, giving me a big grin. Then she surprises me by offering me a double shot of something with whipped cream.

I take it gingerly. "And that is?"

"A buttery nipple," Hazel says, biting back a laugh.

"This is the most action I'll get all night, is that what you're saying?" I ask, cracking up. "God, this is depressing." I take the shot quickly, then begin to zip back to the bar. That was delicious. And I need more delicious in my life.

"Slow down, girl," Hazel says. "You've had plenty of alcohol in a short amount of time."

She's right, the alcohol burns my belly and I should get on the dance floor to sweat some of it off.

Maybe I'll go grind up against a stranger. I don't care. I'm so sick of this same conversation about Charlie. If he doesn't see how amazing I am, then forget him. Even Hazel could see straight away that I was awesome.

Apparently, my desire for Charlie was pretty obvious to the new girl in town because she called me out on my crush day one. And if it's that obvious, how can Charlie be so oblivious about it?

As we wind our way through the crowded bar, I can't help but think about what she's suggested. That I pull on my big girl panties and tell Charlie how I actually feel. On the dance floor, I focus on my terrible dance moves--we're talking the helicopter and the moonwalk.

And for a second, I am lost in the moment. The music and the lights and the people all around, but then I catch sight of Charlie over by the bar. Charlie with his massive biceps and dreamy eyes. The jeans that hug his ass *just so*, his cocky smile that tells everyone he meets that he knows just how hot he is, and the beard he knows gets women all over this town hot and bothered.

And it isn't just the way he looks that turns me on. I remember being eight years old and my kitten was stuck in a tree and Charlie climbing it without being asked and saving Petals. He saved my cat. How could I not have fallen in love with him? He was always there, a constant in my entire life, always at the house hanging out with Luke and Clive.

And if I do say so myself, I did a pretty good job keeping my unrequited love on the down low.

But at some point, some other woman is going to realize how amazing Charlie is. They'll see what I've always known. That underneath his man cake façade, he's actually a guy who saves kittens from trees. Some other girl is gonna sweep into town and realize what a catch he is.

And then what will I be left with?

Maybe I should do it. Just like Hazel said. Man up and say what I want.

Him.

I look over at the bar and see a group of 21-year-olds in booty shorts and crop tops hanging on his every word.

Why should one of those girls go home with him tonight? I'm the one who has known him forever.

If Greta can grind against a stranger on the dance floor, then I can make a move on the man I've known for practically my entire life.

I start power walking over toward him, but then my head starts to spin and it's not the alcohol. I can handle my liquor. This dizzy spell is the fact that I am actually gonna go ask for what I want.

Charlie.

I spin back to the bar to order a glass of water but then know I am getting too rational. "Actually," I say. "Another round of beers."

I need to lose my inhibitions if I want to get where I want to go.

With a few shots in hand, not-exactly tipsy AF, but

definitely power walking to the man I've always been head over heels for.

I pass the dance floor where Greta is wiggling her ass. "Where have you been?" she hollers as I pass her.

I just smile and raise my stein. "Prost!"

The bar hollers along with me, everyone seeming to be looking for a reason to let loose too. The full moon isn't out, but it feels like we are howling to something. Needing something.

I know I am.

"Hey," I say to Charlie and Clive. I push my way past those booty-short girls. This is my stomping grounds and my Oktoberfest more than it is the out-of-towners'. They scowl and walk away, air-kissing Charlie as they leave. Good riddance.

I hand Charlie a beer. He takes it with a devilish grin. Damn, his smile gets me all hot and bothered, and that is not just the booze talking. "To taking a chance," I say.

We clink glasses and chug them like we're college kids.

Clive butts into my moment. Not that Charlie seems to notice this was when the stars are supposed to align. "Where's my shot of something good?" my brother asks.

"Out on the dance floor," I tell him, wanting to get him away.

He grins. "Gonna go find my woman," he says.

With him gone, I look back at Charlie. Pulling up any seduction skills I may have garnered over the years, I go for the kill.

"It's hot, wanna get some fresh air?"

He cocks his head, and for a split second, I think he is going to say no, that he is going to grab a co-ed and take her outside. But he surprises me.

"Do you have the keys to your bakery on you?"

I raise a brow. "Yeah, why?"

"After all this booze, I'm dying for a cupcake."

I bite my bottom lip, nodding. This is going better than planned. "I have some frosting you've never tasted before. Want to come to try it?"

He jumps off a barstool; his hand is on the small of my back as he leads me outside. He doesn't know the plan I've baked up--but I'm hoping it gets a rise out of him before he realizes what I'm up to.

About the Author

Frankie Love writes filthy-sweet stories about bad boys and mountain men.

As a thirty-something mom to six who is ridiculously in love with her own bearded hottie, she believes in love-at-first-sight and happily-ever-afters.

She also believes in the power of a quickie.

Find Frankie here:
www.frankielove.net

Printed in Great Britain
by Amazon

24353470R00061